the Dudgeon is coming

Lynley Dodd

'Pass on the news,'
said the bombazine bear
to the taffeta cat
who was dressing her hair,
'The Dudgeon is coming,
he's shy
and polite . . .

'Look after the Dudgeon –
he's coming
tonight.'

'Pass on the news,'
  said the taffeta cat
  to the hopalong snoot
  in a ten-gallon hat,
'The Dudgeon is coming!
  He isn't polite . . .

'Look out for the Dudgeon –
he's coming
tonight!'

'Pass on the news,'
said the hopalong snoot
to the blue cockatoo
who was knitting a suit.
'The Dudgeon is coming!
He'll give you a fright . . .

'Take care,
for the Dudgeon is coming
tonight!'

'Pass on the news,'
said the blue cockatoo
to the stickleback twitch
in his bamboo canoe,
'The Dudgeon is coming!
He's likely to bite . . .

'Stay clear of the Dudgeon –
he's coming
tonight!'

'Pass on the news,'
  said the stickleback twitch
to the pineapple pig
  in her mudwallow ditch,
'The Dudgeon is coming!
  There might be a fight . . .

'Beware of the Dudgeon –
he's coming
TONIGHT!'

'Pass on the news,'
said the pineapple pig
to the omnibus owl
in his Regency wig,
'Warn everybody
with all of your might . . .

'THE TERRIBLE DUDGEON
IS COMING
TONIGHT!'

Then came a swish
and a shiver of leaves,
a soft pitter-pat
through the shadowy trees.
A very small voice – like a bumblebee hum – said . . .

'Hi,
I'm the Dudgeon.
I've finally
come!'

PUFFIN BOOKS

Published by the Penguin Group: London, New York, Australia,
Canada, India, Ireland, New Zealand and South Africa
Penguin Books Ltd, Registered Offices: 80 Strand, London WC2R 0RL, England

puffinbooks.com

First published in New Zealand by Mallinson Rendel Publishers Ltd 2008
First published in Great Britain in Puffin Books 2008
Published in paperback 2009
1 3 5 7 9 10 8 6 4 2
Copyright © Lynley Dodd, 2008
All rights reserved
The moral right of the author/illustrator has been asserted
Made and printed in China
ISBN: 978-0-141-50216-8